MICHAEL DAHL'S
REALLY SCARY STORIES

Michael Dahl's Really Scary Stories
are published by Stone Arch Books
A Capstone Imprint
1710 Roe Crest Drive
North Mankato, Minnesota 56003
www.mycapstone.com

Library of Congress Cataloging-in-Publication Data is available on
the Library of Congress website.

ISBN: 978-1-4965-3772-0 (library binding)
ISBN: 978-1-4965-3776-8 (ebook PDF)

Summary: A game of tag turns monstrous one night in the forested
village of Pine Bluff, where kids who are It for too long transform
into something terrifying. When little Mateo goes missing after being
It, the kids begin to worry who the next victim will be — only to
discover that the truth may be scarier than they thought! Follow
along with Mateo and others in this collection of scary stories.

Designer: Hilary Wacholz
Image Credits: Dmitry Natashin

Printed in Canada.
032016   009647F16

THE BOY
WHO WAS IT
AND OTHER SCARY TALES

By Michael Dahl

Illustrated by
Xavier Bonet

STONE ARCH BOOKS
a capstone imprint

TABLE OF CONTENTS

Dear Reader,

Not long ago, my mother heard a ghost. Or a monster. She's not sure which.

My Aunt Tiny's house has been the site of a lot of strange happenings lately. Mist gliding through hallways, doors opening on their own, phantoms putting on their gloves in the basement. Yup, it's true.

When my mother went to visit, she went on a bright, sunny day. That didn't stop the ghostly activity. A deep, guttural sound came from the basement while my mother and Aunt Tiny were drinking tea. Someone, or something, was clearing its throat.

I don't know how they were brave enough to finish their tea, and not run screaming from the house.

I guess everyone has a dash of **COURAGE** in them. Courage they may not even know they have. You'll need that courage now, when you turn the page and start to read . . .

Michael Dahl

THE
ELEVATOR
GAME

It was after school, and Leo and Sam were riding the city bus home. Their families lived in apartments downtown, so they didn't take the regular school buses like everyone else did. The city bus was always crowded, and it stopped at every block. By the time the boys got home, it was usually dark.

"Have you heard of the elevator game?" Sam asked.

"Is that the one with the spooky lady?" asked Leo.

"Yeah," said Sam. He lowered his voice. "They say a woman fell down an elevator shaft and died. Her ghost is all bloody, and she haunts anyone who rides in an elevator."

"Anyone?" said Leo.

"Anyone who follows the three rules of the game," replied Sam. He had read about them on the Internet.

"Rule number one, you have to use the elevator after people go home from work," he said. "Rule number two, you have to pick a building that has at least fourteen floors. And then —"

"Why fourteen?" asked Leo.

"Because the fourteenth floor is actually the thirteenth," said Sam. "Lots of buildings don't count the thirteenth floor because the number thirteen is bad luck. Instead, the floor numbers go from twelve to fourteen."

"Have you done it?" asked Leo.

Sam stared at his friend. Then he looked out the bus window at the tall office buildings. Some windows were still brightly lit, but others were already dark. "Not yet," said Sam. "But I know some kids who did it. You remember Raymond Garcia from Mr. Barker's class? His family had to move away because Raymond saw the ghost. His hair turned white, and he couldn't speak. Now he's in a hospital all the time."

Leo looked at Sam, but the other boy wouldn't look him in the eye. *Just a story*, thought Leo. If that Raymond kid couldn't talk, how did they know what happened to him?

"So which building did Raymond go to?" asked Leo.

"The Graver," said Sam.

The bus wheezed to a stop at a busy street corner. More passengers got on.

"Hey, this is 8th Street," said Leo. "I gotta go." Leo grabbed his backpack, jumped up from the seat, and swung out the side door.

"Wait!" said Sam. "I didn't tell you about rule number three —"

Leo was already outside when Sam finished talking. He waved at Sam's pale face in the window. Sam's eyes were big and he was mouthing some words. *Don't look at . . .*

"What?" Leo asked. He cupped his hand to his ear.

The bus roared and pulled away. *What did Sam say?* Leo asked himself. *Don't look at her? Don't look at* who?

On the sidewalk, a flood of gloomy workers surrounded Leo. He had never seen so many. The murmuring crowd shoved him first one way, then another. He almost lost hold of his backpack. He was turned around so many times that he finally he lost his sense of direction. He couldn't even see a street sign.

Leo forced his way out of the mob. He leaned against the side of a building to catch his breath. Something bony pressed against his back. He turned and saw metal letters jutting out from the wall. GRAVER BUILDING.

Sam felt his skin prickling. This was the building. He walked over to the glass doors and gazed in. The lobby looked deserted. Only a few lights were still on. There was a guard sitting at a desk, but he was sleeping.

Leo hadn't planned on trying that stupid game, but something was pulling him into the building. It was almost as if he couldn't help himself.

It was just a game, after all. Leo wanted to prove to Sam and everyone else that the story about Raymond was fake.

There is no such thing as ghosts, Leo told himself. *Especially here. Ghosts haunt old houses, not office buildings.*

Leo stepped into the lobby. He saw two old-fashioned elevator doors near the back.

He quietly walked toward the elevators and pushed the up button. Above each door was a row of lights, indicating which floor the elevator was on and if it was moving. The one on the right was stuck on the fourteenth floor. The one on the left was moving quickly toward the lobby. Eighth floor, seventh floor, sixth floor —

When the elevator on the left reached the lobby, the door slid open. No one was inside.

Leo hesitated for just a moment. Then he rushed inside before he could change his mind. He pushed the button for the fourteenth floor, and the door slid shut with a hiss.

Smoothly, the elevator rose, dinging as it passed floor after floor. When it reached the fourteenth floor — really the thirteenth — the door opened. No one was waiting for it. *All the workers must be gone,* Leo thought. He stepped out of the elevator for a quick look around. The sound of a vacuum cleaner came from the end of the hall. *Must be a maintenance worker cleaning up for the night.*

Hiss! The elevator door slid shut.

Leo turned around. He reached for the down button that was on the wall between the two doors, but then he noticed something. The elevator on the right, the one that had been sitting on the fourteenth floor all along, was still there. The door was open.

Leo stepped inside. He pushed the button for the lobby and waited. The door closed without a sound.

Well, that's that, thought Leo. *Now I can tell Sam his story was a fake. Just one of those dumb urban legends that everyone talks about.*

The elevator stopped on the seventh floor. The door opened onto a dark, silent hallway. No one was there.

Leo punched the lobby button again. *Hiss,* and the elevator descended once more. He watched the lights above the inside of the door. Sixth floor, fifth floor, fourth floor . . .

The hum of the moving elevator grew to a loud groan, and then suddenly went silent. All the lights went out. Leo felt the elevator grind to a stop.

Leo could see nothing. He heard a soft noise from somewhere behind him. Someone was breathing. *Or is that my heart beating?* Leo wondered. He reached blindly toward the buttons. When his hands reached them, the plastic buttons were icy cold. He slapped at them wildly, hitting as many as he could.

Zhooom!

Suddenly, the elevator jerked and started moving again. The lights snapped on.

Leo whipped around to see where the breathing sound was coming from. He was alone. Leo thought, *I'm just letting Sam's story get to me.* He swallowed hard and adjusted the backpack on his shoulders. He would be glad to get out of there. The elevator came to a smooth stop and the door slid open.

"What!" yelled Leo. He wasn't at the lobby.

Instead he found himself in a dark gray hallway. It looked like a basement.

"Stupid elevator," he said impatiently. "I'm never getting out of here."

"Oh yes, you will," a voice whispered behind him.

A tall woman stood in the corner. Long black hair covered her face. Her clothes were torn and burned.

She reached a thin white hand toward Leo. He cried out and bumped up against the wall. The white hand moved past him to press the button for the lobby. Leo watched, frozen, as the door closed quickly.

"Don't worry," the woman whispered. "You won't be here long." Her straight black hair seemed to move like curtains in a night wind. "What's the worst that could happen?" she asked.

Then the lights went out.

BUMP IN THE NIGHT

Violet got a Skype alert in the middle of the night. After she got out of bed and walked over to her computer, she let out a groan. Why was Jane calling her? Her little sister was supposed to be sleeping over at a friend's house. And why wasn't she using her phone?

Violet clicked the "accept call" button. As soon as little Jane's face came onto the screen, Violet snapped, "Why are you bugging me?"

Jane looked upset. "Violet, you have to come over here now!" she cried. "You have to come help me!"

Violet was a little bit concerned, but she figured her little sister was just homesick. "You'll be fine, Janey. I'm going back to bed."

"But something bad is happening. Really bad," Jane said. "You know how Victoria said her house was haunted by a bump in the night? Well, it is! And it's a big bump!"

"Old houses make weird noises at night," Violet said matter-of-factly.

"No," said Jane. "I don't mean a bump like a noise. I mean, a *bump*! Like a lump. A lump of something under the rug."

"Hah!" Violet said. "Did you have too much candy tonight? You must be dreaming."

"No, I mean it!" Jane shouted. "We were watching a scary movie —"

"See?" interrupted Violet. "You're having a nightmare."

"I'm telling the truth, Vi," Jane said seriously. "We saw part of the living room rug start to rise, like something was underneath it. Like when the cat gets under the bed sheets, you know? And then Victoria's dad yelled, 'It's here again!' And everyone in the house ran to their rooms."

"So then where's Victoria?" asked Violet.

"I don't know!" said Jane. "The bump was chasing us, moving under the rug really fast. When we got to the hall, there was no rug. The bump kept coming, only it was under the wood floor this time. We ran up this big old staircase, and it kept following us. Then somehow it slid up the wall and was moving under the wallpaper! It never stopped. I made it to Victoria's bedroom, and she was supposed to be right behind me. That's when I heard her scream."

"Who scream?" Violet asked, sounding bored.

"Victoria!" Jane yelled. She was sounding more and more panicked. "Aren't you listening to me? She's gone! I'm locked in her room. I'm using her computer, because I left my phone downstairs. I'm thinking if the bump can move under wood or wallpaper, it must be able to squeeze under a door . . . oh, no, look!"

Jane must have turned Victoria's computer camera in a different direction, because now Violet was looking at another part of Victoria's bedroom.

"Do you see it, Vi? Do you see it?" Jane asked.

Violet's screen was dim. It was hard to see anything. She thought she saw a dark shape next to a door, but she couldn't be sure. She shook her head slowly.

"It's the bump! It's here! It's in the room!" Jane yelled.

Violet's computer screen went blank. The Skype session ended. Violet sat back in her chair and stared.

This was a prank, she decided. Jane and Victoria were pranking her. Or else her little sister was having a nightmare. A bump in the night? How stupid was that?

Pop!

Something next to the wall sizzled and sparkled. Violet saw tiny sparks fizzing out of the plug where her computer cord was attached to the outlet. *It must be short-circuiting*, she thought. Then, slowly, the cord next to the wall expanded like a balloon.

It was the bump.

The bump traveled along the cord. It moved closer to the computer sitting on Violet's desk.

Violet jumped up from her chair and stood, watching, unable to move, unable to believe what she was seeing.

The bump inside the cord moved closer and closer. It reached the computer. Then it disappeared. The cord was back to its normal size.

What is going on? thought Violet.

Now the computer was expanding. The keyboard stretched up and out. The screen grew larger and rounder. White shapes that looked like teeth formed around the edge of the screen. They grew longer and sharper as the computer grew larger.

Violet stepped back.

The bump that used to be a computer grew so large it forced the girl into a corner of her bedroom. She couldn't move. The last thing she saw was Jane staring out at her from deep inside the computer screen with wide, frightened eyes.

THE LOOSE NAIL

Austin O'Connor looked up from his comic book and stared out the car window. They had been driving for hours, but all he had seen was hills and grass. More hills and more grass. This time he noticed a few trees. Then, his father turned onto a dirt road, and Austin immediately unbuckled his seat belt.

Mrs. O'Connor glanced over her shoulder from the front seat.

"Keep your seat belt on," she told Austin. "I know we're not on the main highway anymore, but driving is still dangerous."

Austin thought his mother worried too much.

"And remember," said Mr. O'Connor, not taking his eyes off the road, "Grandma gets very lonely way out here."

"She hasn't seen you since you were a baby," added his mother, smiling.

During the long drive, Austin had realized he couldn't remember actually seeing his grandmother. Only pictures of her. She didn't have a computer and only used an old-fashioned landline phone. In fact, he wondered why they were visiting her now, after all this time. His parents didn't say anything about a birthday. Was there a special reason for driving all the way out into the country?

"Yes, she's quite lonely," his father said. "And sometimes lonely people do, uh, different things."

"What do you mean, different things?" asked Austin.

"Oh George, really!" said Mrs. O'Connor.

"It's true," said Mr. O'Connor. Then he glanced at Austin in the rearview mirror. "Your Grandma has . . . hobbies to pass the time."

"Everyone has hobbies," said Mrs. O'Connor.

"All I'm saying is, if Grandma seems a little different," continued Austin's father, "just remember that she doesn't get a chance to see people a lot. Real people, that is."

The car made another turn in the winding road. Austin saw an enormous old farmhouse surrounded by birch trees and a wide green lawn. His father pulled the car to a stop in front of the house.

Austin and his parents climbed out of their car. His mother leaned in and grabbed a large tote bag that had been sitting by her feet. It looked heavy. "I can carry that," said Austin.

"No!" his mother said sharply, pulling the bag to her chest. She put on a quick smile. "It's fine, dear. I can manage myself, but thanks for offering."

An old woman greeted them from the porch. Austin waved back. "Hi, Grandma," he said. He walked up the front wooden steps and found himself in a soft, warm embrace.

"Oh my, you've grown so much," said the old woman, her tiny wrinkled face close to Austin's.

"How are you, Mom?" asked Mrs. O'Connor.

"You've done such a good job raising your boy," she replied. "I can tell. Just look at him."

Austin was looking at the wide lawn. He couldn't see the main road, hidden a mile away behind walls of trees.

"Sure is quiet here," said Austin.

"And so much to do," said Grandma. "My family keeps me so busy. And my knitting, of course."

"Family?" asked Austin. "But I thought you lived all alone out here."

Austin's mother gave him a shushing look, but it was too late. Grandma was opening the front door and waving Austin inside.

"Before we have lunch on the porch," she said, "you must come in and say hello."

Austin's eyes took a moment to adjust from the bright sunshine outside. He stood in a large dim room that was crammed with a forest of furniture — chairs, tables, cabinets, ottomans, and sofas. At first, Austin thought everything was covered with blankets and pillows. Then he realized they were people. People knitted from yarn.

Some yarn people sat on the chairs with smaller yarn figures on their laps. A family of dolls was squeezed together on a sofa. Other dolls sat at the tables, with cups of coffee in front of them. A couple of yarn kittens perched on windowsills.

"Did . . . did you make all these?" Austin asked.

Grandma smiled. "Of course, dear. That's Grandma's job."

Austin crept over to a boy-shaped yarn figure sitting on a low stool. The figure was the same size as he was. Realistic-looking yarn ears were sewn to each side of the head. Austin put out a hand to touch it.

"I see you're making a friend," said Grandma.

Austin pulled his hand away. The yarn ear had twitched! Slowly, the yarn boy's head turned. One of its arms reached toward Austin. Austin yelled and backed away. Then he noticed that several of the bigger yarn figures were also turning to look at him. A doll at one of the tables knocked over a coffee cup. He thought he heard a gasp from one of the knitted mouths.

"Well, aren't you going to say hello to your cousins?" said Grandma. "After all, this is a family reunion."

Austin screamed and ran out the front door. He raced across the porch and down the wooden stairs. He did not see the loose nail sticking up from one of the steps.

"Austin!" his mother shouted.

Faster and faster the boy ran. He had to get away. Something wasn't right. How could the dolls move like that? And what did Grandma mean when she said they were his cousins?

Austin kept running. He wouldn't stop until he reached the main road. Suddenly, he fell to the ground. He looked down and saw, below his shorts, his left leg was missing. In its place was a long flesh-colored strand of yarn, winding all the way back to the front porch and to the loose nail that had caught against Austin's foot.

"Austin!" He heard the old woman's voice. She was walking across the grass, winding up the string of yarn into a ball as she went.

"Dear, dear," she said. "You'll have to stay with me for a while. I can't have you go home looking like that."

The old woman looked off into the clouds, her thoughts far away. "I remember when I first made you for your mother. The poor dear couldn't have children, so I helped out. I love knitting. And you made her so happy." Then she turned to glance back at her distant house. "It's a good thing your mother brought all that extra yarn with her," she said. "You need to grow a little more before school starts again. We want you just as tall as the other boys."

ERASED

Thunder boomed outside the classroom, and Mrs. Denton raised her voice to be heard. "Quiet, class. We've all heard thunder before. Everyone get out your drawing pencils."

Holli opened the lid of her desk. She was about to grab the colored pencils she always used for art class, but a metallic gleam caught her eye.

I forgot all about this, thought Holli, reaching in and pushing aside some papers.

For her birthday two months ago, Aunt Olive had given her a pencil box with an orange dragon on the lid. The dragon was blowing fire. Holli picked it up and followed the swirls of gold and yellow flame onto the back of the box. When she turned the box back around, the dragon was gone. Instead, swooshes of orange fire decorated the front. *Weird,* thought Holli. *Maybe I just thought all those swooshes looked like a dragon.*

Holli popped opened the lid. The smell of burnt caramel swirled into her nose. Inside were twelve colored pencils and a bright red eraser printed with the words "Magical Eraser." The words seemed to wiggle, like waves of heat off of pavement in the summertime.

Another rumble of thunder shook the room as Mrs. Denton opened her mouth to speak again. "Before you begin drawing," she said, "describe what you see. Write down a sentence and tell us what you are looking at."

The boy sitting in front of Holli raised his hand. "What do we look at?" he asked.

"Good question, Russell," answered Mrs. Denton. "Look at anything at all. It could be something from your desk, something in the room. Or even outside the windows."

Holli looked outside. There was not much to see. Dark clouds had filled the sky. Lightning flashed and thunder rumbled. Tree branches bent in the wind.

She started writing with the new brown pencil: *The girl watched the lightning through the window and listened to the thunder.*

Holli rubbed her nose and frowned. *Boring,* she thought. Mrs. Denton was always teaching them to use "vivid language." How did the lightning flash? How did the thunder sound? How did the girl feel as she watched the storm?

She grabbed the eraser from the pencil box.

"Ow!" she exclaimed. She dropped the eraser onto her desk. A few students turned to look at her. The eraser had felt hot, like the buckles on her backpack when she left it lying in the sun. Holli stared at the bright red block of rubber. She carefully touched it with the tip of her finger. But now it was cool.

Holli picked up the eraser and looked at the sentence. She decided to start over, and began erasing the sentence from the end. First the period, then the word "thunder."

A few rows away, a student gasped. "The thunder stopped!" she whispered. Several students around her mumbled and raised their heads to listen.

Holli didn't notice them. She was busy erasing her sentence: *The girl watched the lightning through the window and listened to the*

She rubbed out the next four words. When she erased the word "window," a girl cried out, "Mrs. Denton! Where's the window?"

Holli looked up. The constant thunder had stopped rumbling. The window on the side of the room was gone. Instead of glass there was a brick wall painted beige, like the other three walls of the classroom. Mrs. Denton stood at the front of the room, her mouth hanging open, staring at the new wall.

A flash of lightning startled the class. A cold fear prickled Holli's scalp. How could there still be lightning without a window to see it through?

More and more students started shouting.

"Where's the window?"

"What's happening?"

"I want to go home!"

Holli looked down at her shortening sentence, then at the eraser in her hand. *That's impossible,* she told herself. *It's just an eraser.* Carefully she rubbed out the next two words — "through the" — but nothing happened. She started on the next word, and as soon as she had erased the letters *ning*, the lightning stopped. The students' cries and shouts grew quieter. The panic seemed to melt away.

Mrs. Denton looked more relaxed. "All right, class," she said. "Let's settle down. I'll call the custodian about the window —"

Without thinking, Holli continued erasing the sentence. The word "light" disappeared, and suddenly the classroom was wrapped in darkness.

Screams and shouts surrounded Holli. She heard the scraping of chairs and desks as students jumped up in fear and began to run. She couldn't see anything. But she still had her pencil and eraser. If she wrote the word "light" again, would everything go back to normal?

Someone bumped into her desk. Startled, Holli dropped both her pencil and her eraser. She heard the metal pencil box clatter on the vinyl floor. The screams grew louder. Mrs. Denton was weeping somewhere in the dark.

Holli dropped to her knees and quickly felt around on the floor. If she could just find that pencil. Legs and shoes brushed past her. No light could enter the room without the window, and with all the students running and stumbling it made it harder to find the way out.

All those feet running and shuffling and tripping past her. What if someone stepped on the eraser? What if that red block of rubber got trapped beneath a shoe? A shoe that was moving, running, rubbing the eraser against the floor? Rubbing and rubbing . . .

Oh, no, thought Holli. *Not the floor!*

Suddenly, everything in the room — desks, chairs, books, pencils, and backpacks — and everyone began falling . . .

Falling . . .

Falling forever into unending darkness . . . a darkness without a floor . . .

HELLO
DARKNESS

The three girls heard the whimper of the puppies echoing inside the long, dark pipe. They stood at the edge of the park farthest away from the playground and the parking lot. The ground dropped off here and sloped down to a river shimmering in the October sunlight.

"How did they get in there?" asked Caroline.

"Puppies are curious," said Ray. "They probably just wandered in there, and now they're afraid to come out."

"Why would they be afraid?" asked Megan. "If they wandered in, they can wander back out."

The round mouth of the drainpipe poked out

of the grassy hillside. The rest of the steel tube traveled horizontally through the ground, back toward the parking lot and the storm drains.

"Maybe something chased them in there," Caroline suggested.

"I think they're just afraid of the dark," said Ray. She squatted down and peered into the mouth of the tunnel for what must have been the tenth time. "It's really dark in there."

The whimpers grew louder, sadder.

"Poor little things," said Caroline for what also must have been the tenth time.

"Well, we either do something or call for help," said Megan. "What's it going to be?"

Ray stared hard at the mouth of the pipe. "I could crawl in there," she said.

The other two girls exchanged glances. "Are you crazy?" said Megan. "It's dark in there!"

"I'm not afraid of the dark," said Ray.

Caroline shuddered. "I don't like closed-in places," she said. "I'd panic if I climbed in there."

"Let's go get help," said Megan.

"If we do that, we might be too late," said Ray.

Ray looked down at her jeans and decided she didn't care if they got dirty or not. "Caroline," she said, "go grab that rope we saw over by the tennis court. You can use it to help me get back out."

Without a word, Caroline dashed toward the other end of the park. Megan bent over and looked at the pipe. "You don't know how far in they are," she said.

Ray smiled. "It can't be too far. We can still hear them," she said.

Caroline quickly returned with the rope. "When I find them, I'll put them in my backpack," said Ray. "Then you two can pull me out." The girl dropped to her knees. "I'll call for you when I'm ready."

Ray shrugged off her backpack and held it in her hand. "It might be too narrow in there to take it off," she said. Taking a deep breath, Ray turned to the pipe. She squirmed inside. "Wish me luck," came her muffled voice from inside. Her legs quickly disappeared from sight. Before long, the other girls couldn't see the soles of her shoes anymore. The tunnel was too dark.

Both Caroline and Megan were worried about their friend's decision.

After a couple of minutes, Caroline knelt down and yelled, "Are you okay?"

A voice echoed back. "I'm fine. I think I'm getting closer."

The sound of the puppies had died down. Megan and Caroline could hear only a rustling sound that they assumed was their friend.

In a few minutes, Megan called into the pipe. "Ray, what's happening?"

There was no response. "Ray!" she shouted.

The rustling had stopped. The dark tunnel was silent.

Caroline cried, "Ray! Say something!"

A warm breeze ran up the hill from the river below. The grass sighed and the clover flowers danced around them. The two girls watched each other, their expressions worried, as they strained to hear the slightest sound.

A moan echoed from the pipe.

"We're going to get help!" shouted Caroline.

Finally, there was a whisper. "Help."

"Are you okay?" said Caroline. "Do you have the puppies?"

There was a long pause before their friend answered. "There are no puppies," came the whisper.

"What made the sound, then?" Megan asked in a shaky voice.

"It was trying to trick us," Ray whispered from the pipe.

Suddenly, the rope was yanked out of Caroline and Megan's hands. With a sharp snap, the rope lashed back and forth like an angry snake and then disappeared into the drain. The two girls jumped up and screamed.

The sound of the thrashing rope grew fainter and fainter. Then a whisper followed.

"You can't . . . help," came the distant girl's voice. "It's too strong. You have to . . . run . . . run now!"

A thunderous rumble came from inside the pipe. Caroline and Megan turned and ran down the slope.

Neither girl looked back. Neither girl saw the wide, inhuman face filling the space of the tunnel's mouth. A face that licked its slobbering lips and then slid out of the pipe like an enormous shadowy serpent, following the screaming girls as they raced toward the river.

THE BOY
WHO WAS IT

The sharp slice of moon, curved like a grin, hung above the neighborhood trees. Below, in the uncut grass among the maze of trees, Bennie and his friends ran and hid and screamed.

"You're It!" shouted one.

"Now you're It!" cried another.

Back and forth, the game of hide-and-seek combined with tag had been going for hours. Bennie had only been It once. He was perhaps the fastest runner among his friends. Poor Mateo had been It a dozen times.

Finally, Mateo stopped. "I hate being It."

The group of friends stopped leaping and laughing. They moved in toward Mateo.

"Being It is fun," lied Robert.

"No, it's not," said Mateo. "It's not fair."

"Well, at least you're not really *It*," said Bennie, with a grin.

All his friends, including Mateo, turned to stare at him.

"Not really It?" echoed Mateo. "What does that mean?"

"Yeah. You're not the real It," said Bennie calmly. "The reason this game started in the first place. Where do you think the idea for It came from?"

Sara shook her head. "Are you making this up?" she said.

Bennie put a hand to his chest. "Me? Make things up? I heard this story from my dad."

"So, what is . . . It?" Mateo asked quietly.

"No one's really sure," said Bennie. "Some kind of monster or something. A creature like Bigfoot that lives in these woods. My dad read about It in the paper when he was a kid. This It thing always stayed out of sight behind the trees, just like these." Bennie gestured toward the huge elms surrounding them. "He was half-human, half-beast."

"See, Mateo?" said Robert. "Being It is like being a monster. Like, powerful. Mighty."

"Like creepy," said Jess.

"They say the first It was a kid just like us," said Bennie. "A kid who was playing with his friends, then got lost in the woods. Something happened to him. I don't know if he got bit, or was poisoned by plants, or what. But he changed. He got big and hairy. His hands turned into claws. His teeth grew so big he couldn't shut his mouth. He was drooling and hungry all the time."

"Cut it out, Ben!" said Sara.

Bennie tried to look innocent. "I'm just telling you what I heard," he said.

The moon no longer hung overhead. It had sunk below the dark branches of the elms. With the moonlight gone, the woods had grown darker. The friends still stood in a circle around Mateo. Only a siren, far away, broke the silence.

"One more game," said Robert, trying to change the mood. "One more, okay? And Mateo, you're It. So be like a monster when you find us and tag us."

"Okay," said Mateo, shrugging his shoulders.

Mateo shut his eyes and counted to twenty while the other kids scattered. Then he looked up and shouted, "Ready or not, here It comes!" He growled half-heartedly and then disappeared among the trees, looking for his friends.

After a few minutes, another sound echoed through the trees. "Kids! Time to go home!" It was Mr. Lopez, Bennie's dad. He was standing in his backyard, yelling toward the trees. "Time for supper!"

Bennie and his friends slowly marched out of the woods and into the pool of light shining from the Lopez's back door. Robert, Sara, and the others all said their goodbyes to Bennie and his dad, filing around the corner of the house and back to their own homes.

Bennie watched them all leave as he stood at the back door. Something bothered him about their departure, but he wasn't quite sure what.

In the middle of supper, Mrs. Lopez's cell phone buzzed.

"No phones at the table, Mom," Bennie called.

Mrs. Lopez had a serious look on her face as she glanced at her phone. "It's Mrs. Ruiz," she said, getting up with the phone and heading into the kitchen.

Mateo's mom, thought Bennie. And suddenly he knew what had bothered him about his friends leaving after the game. He didn't remember seeing Mateo among them.

Mrs. Lopez returned to the table. "Bennie, was Mateo playing with you tonight?"

Bennie nodded.

"His mom says he hasn't come home," said Mrs. Lopez.

"The kids all left at the same time," said her husband. "Right, Bennie?"

"Uh, yeah, right. But I didn't see Mateo, actually," he said.

"He'll show up," said Mr. Lopez. "Mateo moves a little slower sometimes."

While getting ready for bed later, Bennie stared out his bedroom window toward the wooded lot next door. The trunks of the trees were swallowed in darkness. *Did Mateo get lost somehow?* he wondered.

His phone buzzed. It was Robert. "Did you hear about Mateo?" he said. "Nobody can find him. His parents have been calling everyone."

Bennie couldn't talk. The inside of his mouth felt rough. His tongue felt like cardboard.

"You made up that story, right?" said Robert.

Bennie swallowed hard. "Yeah, yeah, of course. It's just a scary story."

Robert paused. "You don't think that happened to Mateo, do you?" he asked. "Like he got lost or turned into It?"

"It's a story!" said Bennie. "Don't be stupid!" Then he clicked his phone off.

Bennie was unable to sleep that night. He lay in bed staring out of his window, gazing at the dark treetops and the stars beyond.

He heard a growl from outside. He jumped out of bed, ran to the window, and opened the screen. He leaned out into the cool air. There it was again. A growl. And it came from the woods. *A dog,* thought Bennie. Then he heard it a third time. It didn't sound like a dog or any other animal he recognized.

Bennie stared hard at the edge of the woods that bordered the Lopez yard. A faint light spilling from the kitchen windows was just enough to see by. Bennie spotted a shape, something moving between the trees. Something big.

Bennie kept staring, but eventually it stopped moving and he lost sight of the shape in the darkness. He slowly returned to his bed.

While he lay there, Bennie heard another growl. This time he didn't want to get up and look out the window. This growl sounded louder. Closer.

Then he heard something that sounded like the back door opening. He kept his head on his pillow, but his ears were alert and straining to hear. A muffle. A thud. Was something coming up the stairs? *I must be dreaming,* he thought.

A low growl came from just outside his closed

door. A groan. The door handle twitched, and the door slowly opened. In the dim glow of the hall nightlight, Bennie saw the silhouette of a huge and hairy beast. Its long arms reached down to the floor. The face was hidden in the darkness, but Bennie thought he could see two spots of red where its eyes should've been. A strand of drool gleamed in the dim light.

Bennie couldn't move. His body was frozen to the bed. As the hairy body drew nearer he smelled something unpleasant, like food left in the refrigerator too long.

Bennie couldn't help watching the beast as it lumbered closer and closer.

He tried lifting his head. "Mateo," he whispered. "Mateo . . . is that you?"

A low growl shook the bedroom. The tall creature bent over the frightened boy. A hairy paw reached out toward the covers.

Then Bennie saw the beast's toothy mouth form words. "Tag. You're It!"

ABOUT THE AUTHOR

Michael Dahl, the author of the Library of Doom and Troll Hunters series, is an expert on fear. He is afraid of heights (but he still flies). He is afraid of small, enclosed spaces (but his house is crammed with over 3,000 books). He is afraid of ghosts (but that same house is haunted). He hopes that by writing about fear, he will eventually be able to overcome his own. So far it is not working. But he is afraid to stop. He claims that, if he had to, he would travel to Mount Doom in order to toss in a dangerous piece of jewelry. Even though he is afraid of volcanoes. And jewelry.

ABOUT THE ILLUSTRATOR

Xavier Bonet is an illustrator and comic-book artist who resides in Barcelona. Experienced in 2D illustration, he has worked as an animator and a background artist for several different production companies. He aims to create works full of color, texture, and sensation, using both traditional and digital tools. His work in children's literature is inspired by magic and fantasy as well as his passion for the art.

MICHAEL DAHL TELLS ALL

My dad used to work on old cars, repairing and then painting them. Sometimes he'd find things abandoned by the previous owners, and once he found a full-sized mannequin. He brought it home, without warning us, and placed it the living room so we'd suddenly see it and scream. What a great trick! When my aunt and uncle came to visit, he hid behind the sofa and made the mannequin's plastic hand touch my aunt. Every time I saw a trick or heard a scary story as a kid, I think it was filed in a folder in my brain. Now, when I try to write my own stories, those folders fly open and give me ideas. Here's what was inside a few of those folders . . .

THE ELEVATOR GAME

This story is based on an urban legend in Japan. I was reading about elevators, which frighten me, and learned about this game played by young Japanese teenagers. My version of the game is much simpler. But in the original, the ghostly woman, or man, stands there in the corner. I thought it would be scarier for her to interact with the kid who was playing the game.

BUMP IN THE NIGHT

When I was in fifth grade, I read and re-read Nandor Fodor's *Between Two Worlds* dozens of times, a book full of weird and paranormal events throughout recent history. One of the sections in his book is called "Of Things That Go Bump In the Night." It's an old Scottish phrase referring to any kind of creepy noise that might frighten us while we're in bed. I've never forgotten the saying. And while I was thinking about it not long ago, I thought about the different meanings of that word "bump." And then the story popped into my brain.

THE LOOSE NAIL

Did you know there's a village in Japan filled with life-sized dolls made of yarn? In 2005, a woman returned to her small hometown of Nagoro to find that the population was shrinking. She was lonesome, so she decided to make a yarn version of everyone who had either died or left the village. There are yarn children sitting in an abandoned school house, yarn grown-ups sitting outside their houses, and yarn farm workers standing in lonely fields. There's even a yarn wedding party. Would you want to spend a night in Nagoro? What if a gentle breeze brushed against a yarn figure and made it move? What if the figures moved when no one was looking? I don't know about you, but if I get the chance to visit Japan, I'm taking a trip to Nagoro. But I'm not staying the night.

ERASED

I wrote a book years ago called *The Word Eater* about a monster whose long, sticky tongue could erase words from books or the sides of buildings. When the word disappeared, so did the thing the word described. For example, when the Eater licked a name off a mailbox, the sounds of laughter and conversation inside the house vanished. The family disappeared. Recently, a friend of mine wrote a story about a kid who had a magical pencil, and everything the pencil wrote came true. Those two stories collided in my brain and I came up with this "reverse story" about Holli and her eraser. Holli, by the way, is a real person. She and her cool family live in Devon, England. If she has a magical eraser, she hasn't said so.

HELLO DARKNESS

My sister Linda is afraid of drains. My sister Melissa is afraid of monkeys. I am afraid of dark tunnels. What could be scarier than a tunnel that is a drain full of monkeys? Well, there are no monkeys in this story, but something far worse, although it's clever like a monkey. It's something never seen before on our planet. Never seen because it's been hiding deep inside that drain, practicing its voices. The title comes from a Simon & Garfunkel song I liked when I was in seventh grade, "The Sound of Silence."

THE BOY WHO WAS IT

Everyone has played tag or hide-and-seek at night, right? And everyone has been It at some time. When I was eleven, my family lived outside the city on a double lot covered with trees and hedges and bushes, with lots of great hiding places for my friends and me. I often think about those nights and how much fun we had scaring each other. But not until a few weeks ago did I wonder what else might have been hiding in the dark, waiting to play.

GLOSSARY

departure (di-PAHR-chur) — the act of leaving or setting out

homesick (HOME-sik) — sadness due to being away from your family or friends

inhuman (in-HYOO-muhn) — lacking human qualities

innocent (IN-uh-suhnt) — not guilty

mighty (MYE-tee) — powerful

ottomans (AH-tuh-muhns) — footstools

prank (PRANGK) — a playful or mischievous trick

reunion (ree-YOON-yuhn) — a meeting or gathering of people who have not seen each other for a long time

rustling (RUHS-ling) — making a soft, fluttering sound

serpent (SUR-puhnt) — a snake

shadowy (SHAD-oh-ee) — full of shadows, or lacking light

silhouette (sil-oo-ET) — a dark outline of someone or something

unending (uhn-END-ing) — without end

unpleasant (uhn-PLEZ-uhnt) — not pleasing

vivid (VIV-id) — lively or active

whimper (WIM-pur) — quiet, crying noise

DISCUSSION QUESTIONS

1. If Mateo had been the narrator of "The Boy Who Was It," rather than Bennie, how might the story be different?

2. Explain how Austin's grandmother is acting when he and his parents come to visit in "The Loose Nail." Use examples from the text to discuss why you think she is acting that way.

3. If you were Violet in the story "Bump in the Night," would you have believed Jane about the bump? Discuss why or why not.

WRITING PROMPTS

1. Pick one character from this book of short stories and write a paragraph explaining why you would or would not like to have him or her as a friend.

2. Ray goes into a spooky tunnel in "Hello Darkness" and then doesn't come out. Write a short scary story about what happens to her when she goes inside.

3. Describe the setting — the place and time the story happens — of "Erased." What clues did the author give that helped you determine the setting?

MICHAEL DAHL'S
REALLY SCARY STORIES